A Horse Called Dragon

A Horse Called Dragon

Lynn Hall

ILLUSTRATED BY JOSEPH CELLINI

FOLLETT PUBLISHING COMPANY
CHICAGO

To Henry Gregor Felsen,
for having confidence in me.

ISBN 0 695-40134-3 Titan binding
ISBN 0 695-80134-1 Trade binding

Library of Congress Catalog Card Number: 71-121411

First Printing

OTHER BOOKS BY LYNN HALL

Ride a Wild Dream

"A superior horse story with an uncontrived ending. . . ."
SCHOOL LIBRARY JOURNAL

". . . the story of Jon's efforts to win acceptance and to adjust
to life's inevitable disappointments is marked by a realistic
treatment of characters and situations." ALA BOOKLIST

Too Near the Sun
A JUNIOR LITERARY GUILD SELECTION

"The story of a young rebel in a moribund Utopian com-
munity. . . . The plot is sturdy, but it is the pervasive theme
that is of importance: how much individuality should man
sacrifice for the common good, and who is to decide what that
good is? The theme is . . . an integral part of the story. The
setting and the characters are effective and unusual." THE
BULLETIN OF THE CENTER FOR CHILDREN'S BOOKS, UNIVERSITY
OF CHICAGO

The Shy Ones

". . . . A good story with believable characters and much information about the raising and showing of dogs." SCHOOL
LIBRARY JOURNAL

". . . . The satisfying story is valuable for its full, consistent
characterization of the somewhat introspective heroine, with
whom many girls will identify." ALA BOOKLIST

The Secret of Stonehouse

". . . . Heather's fascination with an old stone mansion finally leads to a dangerous encounter and the solution of the mystery of her real identity. Well-built suspense for romantic girls." ALA BOOKLIST

Gently Touch the Milkweed
A JUNIOR LITERARY GUILD SELECTION

Seventeen-year-old Janet Borofen couldn't help but see the likeness of the milkweed to herself—a big-boned, awkward girl, with a plain face and calloused hands. But within the rough milkweed pods there were the soft silver clouds of seeds, and she felt that within her own harsh shell there were also seeds of something beautiful, the seeds of a gentle and sensitive woman.

The Legend.............

No one knows for certain the origin of the Mexican
mustangs, small horses that live in the Sierra Madre
mountains in Michoacán, Mexico. But the generally
accepted belief is that they originated from a handful
of Spanish Barb horses that were being brought to
Mexico to aid in the Spanish Conquest in the Six-
teenth Century. According to the story, the ship carrying the horses was sunk in a storm just off the
Mexican coast, and a few of the horses managed to
free themselves from the wreckage and swim ashore.

Horsemen might raise a questioning eyebrow at
the suggestion that the homely little mustangs could
claim any family ties with the beautiful Barbs, for
today's Mexican mustangs are hardly larger than
ponies, and most are either pintos or appaloosas.

Centuries of near-starvation probably accounted

for their gradual shrinking in size, because the smaller individuals could live on less food and therefore usually survived their larger brothers. Then, too, when the people in this mountain area began to farm the land, they caught and gelded only the larger horses for farm work, leaving the smaller ones free to roam and reproduce.

These people were afraid of any horse whose predominant color was white because they believed the light-colored horses carried evil spirits. So the pintos and appaloosas were left to their freedom long after the solid-colored animals were pulling crude plows.

The changes were great, from Barb to mustang, and yet one quality, more important than size or color, binds them together. It is the quality that enabled that original handful of highly bred and pampered horses to adjust from a world of box stalls and full hay mangers to the incredible hardship of mountain existence. It is the quality of adaptability, coupled with an unconquerable will to live.

Today the mustangs face a greater threat than the mountains ever posed—the inescapable spread of civilization into their wilderness. How will they meet this final test?

Perhaps the answer lies with the small freckled stallion known as Dragon. Insofar as the facts are known about his early life, this is his story.

Courage takes many forms.
The strength to cease fighting
when the fight is wrong
is sometimes the greater courage.

Chapter One............

It was a difficult birth. The mare was old, and months of hunger had drained her strength.

She was small, even for a mustang; her coat was a lusterless brown with white appaloosa markings over her hips. Cakes of mud clung to her legs and straining flanks. Her mane and tail were made, not of hair, but of mats and burrs and dried weed stalks collected on the month-long climb to the Den of the Dragons Canyon.

La Caverna de los Dragones it was called by the few people who cared to call it anything. It was a long winding box canyon in the Sierra Madre mountains of Michoacán, Mexico. The canyon and the horses belonged to the Montenegro ranch, one of the few large ranches in the area, but both canyon and horses were too remote and too worthless to warrant any attention from the owners.

The mare groaned and delivered her foal. From the far end of the canyon, where the caves made black holes in the pink-and-gold mountainside, she heard the whisper of the bats' wings. She raised her head and saw them coming, a darting black cloud against the pale green evening sky, then lowered her head again to the ground. She depended on the stallion to keep the bats away; she was too weak to do otherwise.

As the sound of the bats' wings reached his ears, a small white stallion, flecked with red leopard spots, moved close to the mare and foal. He came reluctantly, resenting the bother of the bats and the new foal and another season of bats and new foals. He took his position near the wet little scrap of life. Slowly his head drooped; his left hip sagged as one hind leg cocked, resting.

The rays of the sinking sun were just touching the mountain peaks as the bats flew close to the new foal and settled in a poinsettia bush to wait. They were vampire bats, known to the local people as *dragones*, and tonight in their search for food, they had come upon the birth, the helpless new life.

A little rested now, the mare climbed to her feet and began to clean the foal. Her tongue went into the tiny ears and nostrils, over tightly closed eyes, and on until every inch of the small body was clean and damp-dried. She wasn't gentle. Finally the foal's

head wove away in protest, and he began to flex his legs. The mare stood aside then, near the dozing stallion, and waited for the foal to get up.

In the poinsettia bush the bats were waiting too, their wings folded about their mouse-brown bodies like opera capes, their needle teeth occasionally showing white against the evening grayness.

The foal was feeling the first sensations of muscle and movement, the pull and flex of all his parts. It had been an exhausting journey out of the close dark security he had known. He lay still, gathering strength that was as new to him as was this wide, scratchy, confusing place.

He rolled into a half-sitting position with his forelegs splayed, then shook his head and blinked. All around him were shades of gray, masses, movement. And sounds. A soft thud, a quiet snorting sound, something else clear and high and far away.

Then a new sound, a quick, whispered whirr. A mass of small shadows enveloped his head, touched him, landed with soft insistence on his neck, bit him!

He swung his heavy head toward the pain. His baby teeth snapped.

Then the stallion was there, driving his long yellow teeth into the cloud of bats. At once they rose and darted away, searching for a quieter source of food.

The foal's neck was dotted with tiny red punc-

12

ture wounds, but his teeth held a scrap of wing membrane.

The colt, later to be called Dragon, was a dazzling chalk-white with just a scattering of small red spots over his back and shoulders. Bracelets of spots circled each pastern.

His first lessons came fast. He learned that his mother's milk always ended before his hunger was satisfied and that the other mares would kick him away if he got too close.

As the weeks went by, there were other foals to gallop with, but only a few. One died at birth; one caught a leg under an exposed tree root and attracted a pair of coyotes; a third was unwise enough to be born when the mare was separated from the rest of the herd. There was no stallion to drive off the bats. The foal died the next day, so weakened from loss of blood that she couldn't stand up to nurse.

When Dragon was a month old and the youngest of the newborns was able to travel, the stallion gathered his family of slat-ribbed mares and foals and led them out of the canyon. He followed the same trail he always followed at this time of the year, east and down, along the rock-strewn bed of an ancient stream. Sometimes the walls of the stream bed crowded in so close that a large horse would have had difficulty passing between them.

The mountain range was made of gray-green bony folds of earth covered with low, sparse trees, spiny bushes, and boulders. There were colorful splashes of Saint John's flowers and jacaranda, but very little edible grass.

As they made their way down the slope, Dragon followed close behind the stallion, arching his neck and tail and cavorting over the rocks. Nothing escaped him, not the rainbow colors where the sun touched rocky walls, nor the jackrabbits and lizards that darted out of the horses' path, nor the new, richer smell of the air outside his canyon. A time or two he tried to crowd past the stallion, but he was nipped for his impudence and forced back to second place.

Late in the afternoon the trail widened to become a small deep valley, green and inviting. A spring bubbled out of the rocks at one end of it and became a stream that split the valley floor. The water was clear and delicious, and so cold that Dragon's throat ached when he drank. He thrust his tiny muzzle deep into the water and snorted, shattering his reflection with the bubbles.

For the next few weeks, while the grass lasted, the mares tore at it every waking moment. Gradually they began producing enough milk to satisfy their demanding babies, and as Dragon's ribs became a shade less obvious, his energy redoubled. For hours

14

at a time he and the other three foals raced around the perimeter of the valley, leaping the stream, pausing to rear and flail at one another in mock ferocity.

Then suddenly the grass was gone, and the herd moved on down the mountain in search of another valley.

Chapter Two...........

Dragon woke slowly, lifted his head from the ground to yawn, kicked out with one hind leg to relish the pull of his hard young muscles. He rolled up onto his feet and shook, sending a cloud of leaves and dust and bits of grass into the air. It felt good, so he flapped himself again, like a wet pup.

He was six months old now. His mane was long enough to lie over, but it was ambivalent; part lay to the right, part to the left, and a few wisps stood upright. His forelock lay flat, though, and his tail reached nearly to his hocks. The summer months had taken away much of the baby roundness of his profile, had added length to his body and an arch to his neck, and the sorrel freckles in his bright white coat were multiplying.

16

Through the summer the herd had moved down the mountainside, valley by valley, until now they were in the foothills. There was a small lake here, and grass that still showed faintly green through the dust.

The lake was little more than a mudhole, treeless and barren, its water so heavy with silt that instead of reflecting the blue of the sky, it gave back somber halftones of mustard and green. At sunset it was red; thunderstorms turned it the color of plums. That morning it was the same tawny shade as the bare earth around it.

Having shaken himself awake, Dragon trotted to the edge of the water, paused, splashed in. It was muddy underfoot and too shallow for swimming, so he traveled in great high plunges, attacking the glitter of the ripples. Then, exhausted, exhilarated, and dripping slime, he cantered back to the others, to his mother and her milk.

As he slowed to a stop beside her, the mare sidled away from his searching muzzle. He followed. Ears flattened, the mare turned and snapped, pinching his flank sharply.

Dragon stopped and stared in hurt surprise. He moved toward her again; she snapped again. When he tried a third time, she swung her hips at him, thrashed her tail, and cocked up one hind leg. There was no mistaking her message. Slowly Dragon extended his nose—and caught the angry lash of her burr-matted tail.

He retreated to watch from a few yards away. Every now and then he shook his toothbrush mane.

Several times that morning he approached the mare and was driven off. He tried one or two of the other mares and got the same response—bared teeth, flattened ears, threatening hindquarters. By afternoon the ache in his stomach was so strong that in desperation he stretched his short neck down the length of his legs and lipped up a tuft of grass. It was bitter, it was dusty, it tasted nothing at all like the milk that was being denied him, but it did take the edge off his hunger.

He took another bite.

In a few weeks the sparse grass around the lake had all but disappeared. It was well past the rainy season, and what growth there was, was dried to a brittle brown. The horses grew thinner. Almost every day there were angry skirmishes over an edible shrub or a mouthful of dead grass.

One night, when the lake was still russet from the sunset, the stallion nipped his family into an unwilling knot and led them away from the lake. Again their trail was a dry creek bed, and again it led east and down.

They traveled single file, the stallion first, Dragon close behind him, the others strung out in their wake. The air was crisp and very clear, and it began to bring Dragon scents that were new to him. He arched his neck and snorted; his breath was chilled to visibility. The sky was dark now, but there was a full moon that etched the creek bed in black and silver and glowed off of Dragon's whiteness. He filled his lungs with cold black air. He danced. He shied at ghosts. He neighed his challenge to the world.

He tried to pass the stallion and caught a kick in the brisket.

Abruptly the walls of the creek bed fell away, and before Dragon's eyes spread a broad, flat meadow, like no meadow he had ever seen. It was a forest of spears that waved higher than his head, and they grew in straight rows.

Behind him the mares lifted their heads eagerly, then galloped past him into the meadow. The singing of the night insects was lost in the crack of stalks and the loud grating of teeth against tough, dry corncobs. Dragon hesitated only an instant before he followed them.

Much later, when the moon had sunk behind the mountain range, the stallion led them back up the creek bed toward the lake. The west half of the cornfield lay in trampled ruins, but for the first time in his memory there was no ache in Dragon's stomach.

All winter the herd subsisted first on stolen corn and later on the stalks. In March they started up into the mountains again. The valleys that they had grazed bare on their way down through the summer were somewhat restored by now, but the horses didn't linger. For three weeks the stallion prodded them on until, in early April, they pressed through the chasm that led into the Den of the Dragons Canyon. The grass in the canyon had replenished itself and would see them through another foaling season.

One afternoon, shortly after the mares had begun to foal, Dragon raised his head from the grass. The stallion was moving toward him, neither hurrying nor stopping to graze along the way. There was something ominous in the old horse's steady, low-headed walk.

The yearling stopped chewing. The weed he had just pulled up swung, forgotten, from his teeth.

The stallion came close, circled, then rushed. Dragon wheeled, but the stallion's teeth raked his flanks. He squealed and kicked.

But the stallion crowded in on him, shoving him, biting at his ears. The two animals, inside their dust cloud, began moving toward the mouth of the canyon, while the bewildered Dragon defended him-

self as best he could from the incomprehensible attack.

When the stallion turned, finally, and trotted away, Dragon found himself outside the canyon. Alone. Three times during the afternoon he approached the canyon and his herd. Each time the stallion barred him.

Finally he quit trying.

The next day he aimlessly began to explore the flutes and folds of the mountainside, but he never went farther than five or six miles from the entrance to the canyon. He found places where there was a little grass. He found a silty but drinkable pool. But he came back to sleep each night just outside the canyon. When the wind was right, he could smell the herd in there, and occasionally he could hear a neigh or the pounding of hooves.

For several days his only companions were small gray-and-pink lizards and a pair of hummingbirds. Then one morning he woke to the thudding of hooves coming out of the canyon. His ears swiveled to the sound; he sent a nicker of welcome. The exile was over.

At the base of the giant boulder that guarded the entrance to the canyon, the thudding dust cloud stopped. There was a brief battle; then one set of hoofbeats retreated into the chasm. When the dust settled, it revealed a yearling colt, a pinto

22

with whom Dragon had raced and played all his young life.

The colt ambled over. Pinto and appaloosa stood a few yards apart, eyeing each other. He was larger than Dragon, but not so well put together. His neck was short and straight, his chest was narrow, and his forelegs toed out slightly.

Head high, ears stiff, Dragon circled him. But the newcomer turned and wandered away and began sampling the shrubs, the grass. There was an air of moving in and taking over about the pinto's actions— a subtle threat.

Dragon's ears went back. He circled the pinto again. Suddenly the spring morning and the glory of his hard young body swelled to the aching point inside the fledgling stallion. He was strong. Unconquerable. And here was a fight. He trumpeted his challenge at the pinto, so loudly that its echo bounced and bounced and bounced.

Startled, the pinto tossed his head, bolted up the steep slope, and disappeared.

The dust rose and settled as Dragon stared in dismay after the departed foe. His muscles ached for the fight, but the enemy was gone. He sent another challenge ringing through the empty air, then turned away to snort his frustration at a small lizard sunning itself on a rock. The creature had slept through the defense of Dragon's territory.

When the herd moved out in June, Dragon followed. He stayed far enough away that the age-dulled stallion was unaware of his presence, but he kept the horses in sight. It wasn't fear of being alone that held him to the herd, nor was it affection for any of the other horses. The mare who had given birth to him was a stranger now, and the stallion was an enemy.

But the freckled yearling felt no desire to leave and roam the hills alone or to steal mares and start a new herd, as did the other outcast stud colts year after year.

This was his herd. He had to stay.

Chapter Three ....

A full moon blew slowly across the sky, turning the cornfield into a silver etching framed by the black velvet of the mountains. In the corn shadows moved, the dark forms of grazing horses. Their rustling, cracking, munching noises floated up through the crystal air to where Dragon stood watching.

He'd followed them at a safe distance, as he had done all autumn on their cornfield raids. Now he stood on an outcropping of rock near the mouth of the dry creek bed, waiting his turn at the corn and enjoying the sight of the herd spread out below.

The colt had changed during the months of his exile. His barrel was compact, his neck well muscled; his head had taken on maturity and a rugged beauty.

He lipped up a spear of dead grass and chewed it patiently. It was going to be a long wait until the

herd was through in the cornfield, and he was
hungry. He lifted his head, breathed in the warm,
sweet smell of the corn, and thrashed his tail with
impatience.

Suddenly he stopped chewing. Far across the
cornfield something moved. Something rustled.
Something smelled of danger.

Dragon's eyes swept the field. Beyond the grazing horses a line of shadows was moving toward
them. Toward his herd.

He trumpeted and plunged down the slope
toward the herd. The old stallion lumbered toward
Dragon, but the colt ignored him. He whipped
around the mares, nipping, shoving, sending them

galloping up the creek bed.

Then the stallion smelled the danger, saw the circle of riders moving toward them. He forgot that Dragon, too, was an enemy, and for a few breathless moments the pair worked together. They churned through the cornstalks, driving the frightened colts toward the mountains.

A dozen horse-and-rider figures were in plain sight now, galloping though the corn, shouting, closing in. The stallion took the lead and headed up the creek bed, the mares and colts streaming in his wake.

At the rear of the herd Dragon pounded, veering after panic-stricken colts and driving his teeth into

their rumps. He longed to charge ahead, to outrun the creatures behind him, half horse and half shouting monster, but instinct told him to keep after the colts, to keep them from scattering.

As he drove the last colt into the narrow creek bed, something hissed through the air past his head. He ducked and swerved, and the snakelike thing fell to one side, brushing his mane. Behind him, he could hear the grunting of winded horses, the creak of saddles, the shouts of men.

The walls of the bed rang with hooves clattering over stone. Gradually the gap between Dragon and the enemy widened. The pursuers' horses were finding the rock-strewn path tricky going in the deceptive light of the moon.

At last Dragon heard them slow to a stop behind him. He stopped, too, and turned to look back. The horse-and-man figures stood close together, the horses' heads low, their sides heaving. One man raised his arms and waved Dragon away in a motion of disgust.

The young stallion was wet with sweat, but his breath came easily. Deep in his wide, dark eyes was a glow of exhilaration. He raised his head and sent a loud neigh ringing down to the figures below. No one answered his challenge. Slowly he turned and cantered after his herd.

When foaling time approached, the mares, with their lone follower, returned to the Den of the Dragons Canyon. This year they traveled more slowly, roamed more carelessly along the trail.

Dragon took up bachelor residence inside the canyon, at the far end, near the bats' caves. He began spending long hours on a ledge of rock that over-looked the canyon floor and the swollen mares below. Although the old stallion knew Dragon was there, he chose to ignore the colt's presence.

Occasionally Dragon trotted down toward the herd for a closer look. Then the stallion had no choice but to defend his monarchy. He rushed at Dragon and drove him off, but his reflexes were noticeably slower this year, and there was little real danger in his threats. Nevertheless, Dragon allowed himself to be run off, just far enough to satisfy the stallion. For now the colt was willing to bide his time.

One night Dragon was roused from a one-eye-open doze. He tested the wind and pivoted his ears.

The bats were in the air, sweeping down the canyon toward him. This alone was no cause for alarm, not to a tough and wily two-year-old, but Dragon caught a quickening beat in the rustle of their wings. He turned toward the herd. Instinct, or some faint scent, told him there was a birth going on.

He moved out at a smooth, fast trot, skimming the rough ground, his mane lifted from his neck by the breeze he made. Overhead, the bats sailed in his wake.

The mare was down already, near a clump of bushes a little distance from the others. Her time was very near. Dragon approached her quietly, lowered his head to hers for an instant, then took up his position as defender a few yards away.

He threw a long, searching look around the canyon floor and saw the old stallion on the far side of the herd. His head hung, his ears sagged, one hind leg was cocked. Dragon snorted and turned back to the mare

Like decorations on a Christmas tree, the bats settled on the nearest bush to wait. The mare groaned and thrashed her legs helplessly against the pain.

Dragon whickered to her. Then, since he could do nothing to help her, he circled the mare's sweating form and placed himself squarely between her and the bats. He stared at them, and they stared back, their tiny pig eyes gleaming.

Dragon moved nearer to them.

Suddenly his ears flattened and he lunged. He snapped, and felt a small body crunch between his teeth. Quickly he shook his head, sending the remains sailing into the bush.

30

The others rose into the air. A handful descended on Dragon while the rest hovered above. Dragon crashed through the bushes, knocking off a few of the gray-brown devils. He spun and trampled one into the dust, then caught another between his teeth.

High on his neck where he couldn't reach, razor teeth sliced his hide. A long, tubelike tongue began to stroke the wound, massaging, coaxing Dragon's blood. He lowered his head and knocked the thing off against one foreleg, crushing it.

Then the night was silent again. The bats were gone, and behind him the mare was struggling to her feet, her season's work done.

Across the canyon the old stallion woke slowly, gazed around him, then started toward Dragon at a heavy trot. The sun was rising now, turning the mountains gold and pink and violet. It was going to be a beautiful, cloudless day.

As he approached, the old stallion gathered momentum. Dragon moved a little distance from the mare and her new foal and waited.

It was time, now.

A few yards from Dragon the stallion stopped, winded from the short gallop. The two moved in a slow circle, testing.

The stallion lunged for Dragon's throat. The colt sidestepped easily, reared, and slashed his sire along the neck. Angered now, the stallion spun and dove, more carefully this time.

It was a muted battle. The song of a dove rose clearly over the thudding hooves and breathy grunts of the two stallions. Nearby, the new foal sneezed as the dust rose and surrounded her.

The two white-and-red bodies collided again and again. Each time, the collision was more one-sided. Each time, the old stallion weakened. Then the pounding stopped. The dust settled, and the old horse moved slowly, stiffly away.

With no fanfare and very little interest on the part of the mares, Dragon assumed leadership of the herd. Every birth that season was presided over by the zealous young monarch; every foal was minutely examined and snuffled over.

When summer came, Dragon led the way down out of the canyon, for the first time at the head of the line. He nipped and herded with self-conscious authority. He arched his neck until it ached, and he did considerably more galloping back and forth than was necessary. Nevertheless, they made excellent time to the first of their summer-long chain of valleys.

As the months passed, the young stallion settled into his role with the ease of a born leader. Through the winter months the herd lived on the sparse vege-tation around the lake, with frequent supplemental cornfield raids. In March they began the pilgrimage to the Den of the Dragons Canyon, for foaling season.

As he led the parade through the chasm into the canyon, Dragon stiffened his ears suddenly and extended his nostrils.

Horses. In his canyon.

Neck arched, mane and tail streaming, he rocked forward in a canter so tightly controlled it was nearly slow motion. His nostrils flared; his eyes raked the narrow canyon floor.

There. At the far end, near the bats' caves. A good-sized herd, at least twenty mares and fillies, blandly tore at the grass that was to see Dragon's mares through the season, grass that belonged to Dragon just as surely as the caves belonged to the bats who inhabited them year after year.

Across the flat muslin-colored ground he came, faster now. The white body lengthened and flattened to the ground. The afternoon air was shattered by his scream.

From within the herd of grazing mares the encroaching stallion appeared. He saw Dragon coming and moved warily to meet him. When the two were a scant length apart, they froze, muscles bunched, eyes riveted, adrenaline pumping.

He was a pinto, narrow-chested, short-necked, rawboned. They stood clenched and waiting while

33

the small humming, buzzing, chirping sounds of the tiny underfoot creatures seemed to be suddenly still. Heat rippled up in waves from the dust floor of the arena. On soundless wings a pair of buzzards came from nowhere and began a slow circling in the empty sky.

The pinto lowered his head a fraction. Screaming his fury, Dragon lunged. They fought, each for his land, his herd, his life. Each called upon the deepest instincts in his brain, the last surge of strength at his command. They spun, dove, fell, and rose, slashed, fought for breath. The time came when Dragon's strength was gone. He fought on, supported only by grim refusal to die.

And, at last, it was the pinto who died. Dragon left the blood-soaked place to the buzzards and plodded, exhausted, toward his new mares.

Chapter Four..........

It was the first of a lifetime of such battles for the small freckled stallion. During the years that followed, marauding stallions threatened his territory and his mares so frequently that his wounds were seldom healed completely before they were once again opened by deadly hooves and teeth.

Some of his challengers were young colts, newly driven from their own herds, who needed only a taste of Dragon's fury to send them clattering away. Others, many of them larger than Dragon and equally crafty, demanded more endurance than he had. Time and again Dragon's will to live was all that kept him from being the one to remain in the dust, to be torn apart by mountain cats and buzzards, while another stallion trotted off with his mares.

The herd grew during those first years of

Dragon's leadership. By taking them farther from the Den of the Dragons Canyon during the summer months, he was able to find better, fresher pastures than his mares had ever had before. His vigilance at foaling time cut down the number of foals' deaths.

The first years were good ones. Maturity brought Dragon an aura of quality seldom seen among mustangs. His coat retained its chalky whiteness, and his body hardened into granite planes.

In the winter of his eleventh year there was less rain than usual in the mountains above and behind the Den of the Dragons Canyon. In March, when Dragon led his procession of foal-heavy mares through the mouth of the canyon, an unfamiliar scent met him.

He stopped, tensed, raised his head to test the wind. Danger lay before them, but not an animal danger. He lowered his head and trotted slowly across the canyon floor. The scent was all around him now. It rose from the strange plants growing where the grass should be. The low, feathery green gigantillo bushes were beautiful, but threatening in some way Dragon didn't understand.

He lowered his head, extended his upper lip to brush a leaf, then drew back. He whirled to drive the mares back out of the canyon, but several were already tearing at the gigantillo. With a warning snort, he dove at one, then another and another in an angry attempt to separate them from the danger he sensed.

But there were too many mares, and they were too frantic with hunger from their long climb to be easily driven away from the lush low greenery. Again and again the greedier fillies and young mares slipped around Dragon to tear at the gigantillo. When the exhausted stallion was finally able to turn the herd and start them back down the mountainside away from the canyon where all their instincts demanded they should stay, seven young mares lay dying among the feather-soft foliage, their bellies distended with the agony of their foolishness.

The poison waited for them in the next valley, and the next. In the fourth Dragon found no gigantillo, but every blade of edible growth had already been stripped away by horses and deer who had also been driven there by the gigantillo.

Exhausted, uneasy, weak from the same hunger that had driven seven young mares to their deaths, Dragon turned his dwindling herd and started them moving again, down the dry stream bed. His instincts told him that foaling time was dangerously near; that he must find a place with enough food to see them through till the foals were all born and big enough to travel; that the mud lake where they had wintered

was too exposed, too close to the ranches, too grazed over; that no place in the territory familiar to him could give his herd what they must have.

Lifting his head as though the still air might give him a hint, he quickened his pace and veered away from the familiar stream bed into a smaller one angling up and to the right.

For two days they moved east through unfamiliar foothills, doubling back on themselves when dead ends blocked their way, stopping as often as Dragon would let them, eating everything that was edible along the way. On the evening of the second day they came to an area of low treeless hills where the grass was sparse but sufficient. The wind that stirred the dust around his legs told Dragon they were dangerously near men, and that another stallion was already there, waiting among the swells of ground for the fight that would mean the death of one of them. But his mares could go no farther. His head sank as he allowed his muscles to relax and take in, from some unknown source, enough strength to meet the battle ahead.

Dragon and his herd remained in the hill area all that summer and the winter that followed, trapped by the insidious gigantillo that spread through every mountain valley that would otherwise have sheltered them. When the hills were grazed bare, the horses moved down into the outlying corn and wheat fields, risking the danger of exposure for hurried feasts that kept the stronger animals from weakening, shrinking, starving. Few foals survived that year.

Early the following spring, in the village of Mendoza just a few miles from the hills where Dragon's herd subsisted, an official government bounty notice was posted, declaring as a public nuisance the small white stallion with red markings who was responsible for extensive crop damage in the Mendoza area.

One who read the notice with special interest was Tomás Carillo, foreman on the Montenegro ranch. He was a large, placid man well over six feet tall, with a shelf of flesh over his belt buckle that he chose to think of as muscle. He wore, as usual, a blue shirt and formerly white pants.

As he stood in the reflected glare of sun on the whitewashed adobe of the Post Office wall, he read, and read again, the notice tacked on the door. A slow grin spread over his face. He could see himself riding into Mendoza leading that little white plague of a horse, taking him right up to the packing plant, collecting the bounty, watching while that thieving mustang went in as a horse and came out as a case of dog food.

No, a better idea. After all the tongue-lashings Señora Montenegro had given him about the crop damage, he was not only going to get a rope on the little son of a gun; he'd get a saddle on him and *ride* him into town. That would make the revenge complete. He laughed aloud and slapped his thigh as he walked toward the battered ranch truck.

Chapter Five...........

It was a hot, sparkling clear spring night, full of the creaking of insects and the scuttering of rabbits. A flat white moon cleared the rim of the mountains and lit a narrow wheat field that wound between sharp-spined hills. It had been a riverbed once, decades ago. Tonight the young wheat, barely six inches high, rippled silvery-green in the wind, a ghost of the dead river.

Dragon stopped at the edge of the field and looked around carefully. He could see nothing, smell nothing, but he was uneasy. Oblivious to real or imagined dangers, however, the mares galloped past him into the wheat. Slowly he followed.

The stallion was a gaunt caricature of the horse he had been a year ago. His spine was a sharp ridge that seemed ready to tear his skin; his eyes were sunken and lusterless. He had just lowered his head to the wheat when a twig cracked behind him. Startled, he flung his head up. A figure was moving in the darkness—a horse and rider.

He snorted the alarm to the mares. Sweeping them up in a flying circle, he led them down the river valley. The ground echoed the thunder of their hooves, and the air was filled with the fragrance of crushed green wheat.

They were running free, leaving the rider behind. But suddenly another figure appeared out of the shadows at the edge of the field. And another and another.

With the mares close behind him, Dragon flattened his belly to the ground. His legs shot out, blurring, swallowing the earth. The riders that flanked the herd began falling back.

When he was far enough ahead of the riders, Dragon veered left, stretching desperately for the cover of the hills. At the edge of the wheat he turned right again and raced along the base of the rock ridge that lined the field. Suddenly he slowed and plunged up the wall. In a sliding scramble he rocked upward, finding footholds where there were none, falling to his knees, clawing his way up again.

Over the top! He turned to watch while the

mares came up, clumsily following his trail. One by one they spilled up over the rim until no one was left below but the riders.

But it wasn't over yet. Instead of heading back toward the ranch, as they usually did after a chase, the men turned and rode along the base of the wall, looking for a safe slope. By the time they found one, Dragon and his mares were gone, but the riders had little trouble picking up their trail.

Men were no longer strangers to Dragon. Several times the past year they had gotten close enough for him to hear their voices and smell their sweat and tobacco smells. But always he had outrun them, or outclimbed or outsmarted them. Now, for the first time, a new feeling, a kind of dread, overrode Dragon's usual cocky enjoyment of the race. The mares were too near foaling. They were too weak. And he was too tired.

Dawn came. Dragon kept the mares moving at a steady trot. Most of the time the men were out of sight, but Dragon knew they were back there. He couldn't take the mares any farther west, into the mountains. There was nothing up there for them to eat but the gigantillo. Gradually he turned them north, then northeast, keeping to the low hills that still had some grass.

All day they moved, stopping to drink at the few places where there was water. That night they rested

44

for a brief time and snatched at the grass. Before dawn Dragon caught the scent of the men behind them and nipped the weary mares into action, heading northeast again.

For three days he led his herd through bony gray-green hills. Each day the gap between them and their pursuers narrowed as the mares, heavy with foal, moved more and more slowly.

On the morning of the fourth day Dragon could see the riders quite plainly, a half mile or so behind them. There were a dozen, mounted on fresh horses and spread out in a wide arc, closing in slowly, confidently.

Dragon galloped to the head of his weary procession. They were in a narrow chasm with walls that rose so steeply no shrubs dared to grow on them. This was unfamiliar territory to the little stallion. He didn't know whether this valley was a trap or an escape; he knew only that he had to keep the mares moving as long as possible.

Abruptly the valley ended in the sheer rock stomach of the mountain. Dragon saw it and wheeled. The riders were there, a solid line of them across the valley, moving in.

Frantically he bolted for the wall, trying to get between it and the last rider. There wasn't room. He turned again and flew around the milling mares. There was no way out.

A rider was coming toward him, passing close beside the exhausted mares. Dragon darted toward the wall behind him. His glance measured the slope, the rocks. He could make it.

But the mares. He spun back toward them, but they ignored him. Their ribs heaved; their legs trembled beneath them. They had run as far as they could.

Dragon hesitated, and in that instant the rope whistled out and settled over his head. Its touch was an electric shock. He threw his meager weight back, but a second rope caught him from the other side. He stopped fighting then, and turned to face his captors.

The man who had thrown the first rope was smiling at Dragon, a dust-caked, weary smile. He was a huge man, whose white pants and blue shirt were so blotched with sweat and dust that they were almost colorless.

"You run us a good race, little horse," the man sang out. "Now let's get you back to the ranch. You goin' to make Tomás a little money, you and your girls." He turned, counted the mares, and grinned. "Okay, boys, let's get started. I have to see a man about a bounty."

On taut ropes between the two larger horses, a heavy-headed Dragon led the procession out of the valley. The mares, from lifelong habit, followed him.

Chapter Six.............

It was yellow dawn when the herd and its outriders plodded down the lane past the sprawling adobe buildings of the Montenegro ranch. The riders kept the mares bunched together behind Dragon as they threaded between pole-and-mud sheds, around piles of miscellany, and through chickens and ducks pecking casually in their path.

At the gate of a high-fenced pole corral Dragon braced his feet and lunged back in a last desperate gesture, but the two horses that held him walked on inside, dragging him as easily as if he were a sack of grain. The mares followed, the riders backed out, and the gate creaked shut.

The instant the ropes were off his neck, Dragon shook his mane and wove among the mares, checking each of them. He trotted around the corral. The walls were stout, and they rose high above his head. There would be no getting over or through them.

A large, rusty tank of water squatted just inside the corral. As soon as the mares discovered it, they crowded around, seeming not to care that it was man's water and not a mountain stream. Dragon snorted, tasted the dust of which his mouth was made, then moved slowly toward the tank.

While his head was lowered to the water, he caught a quick movement above and behind him. He shied and stared. Over the top of the fence came a flash of metal and a shower of long dried grass. He watched warily. Another pile of the stuff came over and fell to the ground. And another.

The mares moved toward the heap that smelled like food, while Dragon stood to one side, where he could keep an eye on the fence. From beyond the wall he could hear men's voices, but he saw only glimpses of motion between the poles. When, finally, he relaxed enough to think about the food, the mares had eaten all but a few stray wisps.

All that day Dragon paced the sunbaked confines of the corral. The mares seemed to accept their new circumstances calmly enough, but to Dragon it was infuriating to be able to see nothing but walls, to move only within the small circle. Still, a small part of his mind recognized that there was food and water here and that, for now, he needn't worry about finding grass.

Next morning the corral gate opened and Tomás slipped inside, carefully shutting the gate behind him.

"How would you like to go to town, little horse?" he called in a pleasant voice. "You and me got some business at the packing plant, and I want the whole town to see you before . . ." His voice trailed off as he began moving slowly toward Dragon's head.

After a brief, dust-choked fight, the freckled stallion found himself roped and tied up short to the pole in the center of the corral. The man was close to him now; the smell of him burned Dragon's nostrils.

Tomás began talking in a quiet voice. Gradually Dragon's ears relaxed, and his eyes lost a little of their hard stare. Suddenly his upper lip was caught! Something thin and sharp twisted it, cut into it.

He threw back his head and opened his mouth at the pain. In a flash of motion another metal thing was jammed in over his tongue. A hand moved toward his eyes, and something jerked over his ears, twisting them back painfully, and yanking at the corners of his mouth.

50

The man backed away then and gave Dragon a chance to taste, to feel, the thing that had wrapped itself around his head. He worked his mouth, and the metal that lay on his tongue clacked against his teeth. He tried to lower his head to brush the things off with his forelegs, but the rope around his neck stopped him.

Before he could collect himself, the man approached again, this time carrying a dark, bulky object that smelled of horse sweat. From the corner of one eye Dragon saw the object rise into the air. He swerved away, but it landed on his back, and part of it struck his right knee with a hollow clunk. Alarmed, he shied around the post as far as the rope allowed, but the thing stayed on his back. The man was talking again, coming close, reaching under Dragon's belly. The horse stiffened and rolled his eyes.

He felt something touch his stomach. It drew up tight behind his front legs. He snorted and circled the post, but couldn't shake the pressure that bound his ribs. At last he stopped.

"That's a good little horse," Tomás puffed cheerfully. "Now we have a little lesson before we go to town."

With a swift motion the man pulled the rope off over Dragon's head, and with another he vaulted

onto the startled horse's back. Dragon froze. He stood, legs braced and ears flattened, while fury mounted inside him.

"Vamonos, amigo," Tomás called, flailing Dragon's sides with his long legs. Dragon called on all of his meager strength and flung the hated burden toward the sky again and again until his legs quivered from the strain. The weight still bowed his spine. He lowered his head and bolted toward the mares, crow-hopping as he ran. But the man was heavy, and Dragon was weak with near-starvation.

He bucked around the corral for three full turns, then slowed to a stop. His legs shook. Lather coated his neck, and blood colored the foam on his lips.

Again Tomás kicked, with legs so long that his heels nearly met under Dragon's narrow ribs. Confused and weary to the heart, Dragon began a crow-hopping lope around the corral.

"Bueno, amigo. You a smart little horse, hey?"

Abruptly the man pulled back with all his weight on Dragon's mouth, stretching the tender flesh almost to the tearing point. In a frantic effort to escape the hurt, Dragon stopped and began moving backward. Immediately the pain ceased.

"Bueno, bueno," Tomás called again. He smacked Dragon heartily on the neck. "Carlos, open the gate! We're goin' to town!"

The gate creaked open, and for the first time in

two days Dragon saw gray-green hills, his mountains, his refuge. He forgot the man on his back and leaped through the opening.

Outside the corral Tomás hauled back on the reins again, but Dragon ignored the pain and galloped across the yard, scattering chickens and dogs. His mountains were out there.

Tomás changed his tactics. He threw all his considerable weight against one rein until Dragon found his head hauled sharply to one side. Unable to do anything else, he turned and galloped back to the corral.

Back again among the sheds and fences, Tomás pulled the horse to a stop. Dragon was trembling all over now with hatred and a weariness he had never known in all his years of outrunning danger in the mountains.

"Carlos," Tomás shouted, "bring me that sack of corn, please. I think I can trade it at Don Esteban's while I'm in town."

With much grunting and grumbling, a small, bewhiskered cowboy dragged a sack of corn through the dust to Dragon's side. Then, groaning mightily, he heaved it up behind the saddle and tied it there.

"All right, it's done," Carlos panted. "But wait now. There's something else." He trotted over to a small shed and came back a few minutes later leading a young pig by a length of rope.

54

"Señora says as long as you're seeing about the horses, have the pig butchered."

Tomás took the rope.

"One other thing." Carlos squinted up at Tomás. "Señora says when you apply for the bounty on the horses, find out if they will pay more if we wait till the mares have their foals. If they won't, then tell them to send the truck tomorrow, because those mares are eating up all our hay."

"Okay," Tomás sang. "Come on, little horse, let's get going." He clamped his legs around Dragon's ribs, and the horse, head lowered in near-defeat, moved down the lane. The pig trotted at his side.

Chapter Seven..........

For the first few miles Dragon rebelled with all the strength he had left against the singing, flapping, shifting weight on his spine. He bolted, and ran into a wall of pain that tore at his mouth. He lay down in the road and rolled in a frantic effort to crush his tormentor, but the man just stepped off as Dragon went down, and jumped on again as Dragon rose.

Their progress toward Mendoza was slow, but the man's high spirits stayed with them, adding ignominy to Dragon's fear and hate.

They came to a small wooden bridge, or what had been a bridge until the last rain washed away its center support and left it sagging and showing daylight between its rough planks. Dragon veered away from the bridge and maneuvered down the creek bank, hampered by the weight on his back that destroyed his balance. The creek at the bottom was so narrow and shallow that even the pig on his rope leash was able to hop across the water with little trouble.

It wasn't until Dragon had climbed up the far bank, dripping mud, that he saw the object in the road, and the man standing beside it. It was higher than Dragon's head, dark, looming, stinking of something so hateful that Dragon's nostrils ached with the smell of it. There was a horse odor about it, too, and wood and leather, but these were almost lost to him in the other acrid smell and the scent of the man. He stopped and began to back away.

Suddenly the man on his back called, "Good morning, señor. Your truck is broken down?"

"Nothing wrong with my truck that a new bridge wouldn't fix. How in blazes does anybody get anywhere in this Godforsaken hole?"

"Ah, you are American! Perhaps I can be of some service? My name is Tomás Carillo, from the rancho of Señora Montenegro."

"Burr, from Texas. Is there another road to Jiquilpan, or am I going to have to cool my heels till some of you boys get in the mood to fix this bridge? Nothing personal," he said in a slightly calmer tone, "but after a few weeks of your roads my temper ain't

57

what it used to be. Why don't you feed that horse ever' once in a while? He looks like a snake run over by Sunday traffic."

The words had no meaning for Dragon, but he sensed the quick hard stares the man shot at him under cover of the casual talk. He raised his head a fraction and sent back a message of hate.

"Ah, señor, I can see you know much about horses. You were perhaps interested in buying this fine stallion? Not that I could part with him, you understand."

In a matter of seconds the pig was tied to the door handle of the truck, and Dragon stood for inspection, stripped of saddle and corn sack.

Burr walked once around Dragon, laughed rudely, but narrowed his eyes as he studied legs, neck, hindquarters. "Probably wormy," he muttered.

"Oh, no, señor. This has been a bad year for our crops. Lots of wild animal damage, so our horses didn't get enough feed. But this little guy, he's sound and healthy. Good-broke, too, but he's got lots of spirit."

"How old?"

Tomás gazed at the sky. "I think maybe six, seven years old."

Suddenly Dragon's muzzle was caught in Burr's expert grip. He opened his mouth against the man's touch, and the man let go.

Burr's voice was even. "The rest of him may be six years old, Carillo, but his teeth are at least twelve, probably more."

"He has fine lines, does he not? You noticed the legs, the set of his tail? He is a pure descendant of the Spanish Barb horses."

"He's descended a whale of a long way then. What's all the little scars on his neck there?"

"Those are bat bites. Los dragones—that's what we call the vampire bats up in the mountains. In fact"—Tomás's voice took on a note of inspiration—"that is what I call my little horse, El Dragon, because he is brave and fast like the dragones. It would break my heart to sell him."

Burr walked toward his truck, paused, turned back for another long look at Dragon's head. Their eyes met. Hate shone in Dragon's eyes; a quickly hidden gleam of interest lit Burr's.

"How much would it take to cure your broken heart?"

There was a silence while Tomás figured the amount the packing plant would probably pay for Dragon, plus the government bounty. "Three-hundred pesos at the very least, and only because I know you would give him a good home."

"Three-hundred pesos, that's what? About twenty-four dollars, our money? He ain't worth the salt to cure his hide, but it don't look to me like he's

60

getting the best of care now. Make it a hundred pesos and I'll take him off your hands."

"Señora Montenegro would pin back my ears if I sold him for a hundred, but I tell you what. Back at the rancho we got twenty mares due to foal to El Dragon, plus six yearling fillies, and for just"—he paused and moved his lips in silent addition—"for just fifteen-hundred pesos they are yours. Plus the three hundred for El Dragon, of course."

"Well, I don't know. I'd have to take a look at them. Don't know what I'd do with all them horses if I did buy them."

In a matter of moments the saddle and corn were again on Dragon's back, and Burr, his pants legs rolled up, boots in one hand and pig's leash in the other, was leading the way across the creek while Tomás and Dragon followed.

A few hours later, back with his mares in the prison-sanctuary of the corral, Dragon heard the new man's voice again. It, and the voice of a woman, came through the close-set poles of the fence. He trotted to the far side of the enclosure and pressed in among the mares, but the voices still grated in his ears.

"Well, Mr. Burr, now that you've bought the mustangs, what will you do with them?"

Enthusiasm, carefully hidden until the deal was

completed, was betrayed now in Burr's voice. "They'll be foundation stock, ma'am. We're developing a brand-new breed of horses up there in the States. Going to be a small Western-type kids' horse that's tough, quick, smart, and gentle. And appaloosa-marked. They've already got a whale of a market for them, but they need a good stallion who can produce the appaloosa color along with all the other qualifications."

"And you think this horse can do that?"

"I don't know, Mrs. Montenegro. If he don't, I can always geld him, break him, get him registered as a POA—that's the name of the breed, Pony of the Americas—and still sell him at a profit. But from what I heard about these horses down here, I figure he'll make the trip worth my while."

"You came here, then, especially to find a horse like this one? All the way from Texas?"

"Yes'm, I surely did."

"Mr. Burr, I believe my price was too low." The voices faded, laughing.

Chapter Eight..........

Early the next morning the corral gate swung open. Dragon tensed, ready to drive the mares out to freedom, but the opening was blocked by the monstrous, stinking thing he had seen yesterday. Its gaping blackness filled the gate and blotted out the mountains Dragon knew were beyond it.

While he studied the truck, several men advanced toward the herd. Suddenly they began shouting, flailing ropes and quirts, charging at the terrified mares. The men worked around behind the herd and began crowding them toward the square of black. Frantically Dragon darted from side to side, trying to stay between the men and his mares and at the same time trying to get past the tightening circle of men. Again and again he dashed between the men, but there was no place to go except to the other side of the corral.

At length the men tied two lariats together and stretched the rope between them, across the width of the corral. In this net the horses were scooped, with no nonsense, across the corral and up into the dark cavern of the truck.

No sooner had Dragon stepped into the darkness than the tailgate slammed up behind him, and there was no escape. His hooves, and the hooves of the mares, rang with a hollow woodenness on the straw-littered floor. He cocked his ears and looked down at the floor under him. Bits of light filtered up between the boards. It felt unsteady under his feet, and he hated it.

Cautiously he moved the length of the truck bed, pressing between the mares. They were frightened, but his presence calmed them slightly. At the front of the truck Dragon found a rack of hay. He snorted, and had just reached for a wisp when the truck roared at him.

He shied back, as did the mares, in a clatter of hooves. The roaring went on. The truck was shaking now, and giving off a smell that seared Dragon's nostrils. He wanted to fight it, but there was no way.

Then suddenly the floor moved under him. One of the mares squealed in alarm. Dragon whickered a reassurance, but his own legs were braced hard

64

against their lurching base. The roar all around him increased, pounding on his sensitive ears and strumming every nerve in his body. After a few minutes he steadied himself enough to look toward the side of his prison. Between the wide-spaced boards he could see flashes of green and bright blue—his mountains, rolling back away from him, the only safety he knew.

He neighed, just once.

The hours were endless. The slivers of sky that flashed past his head turned from blue to black, then slowly to blue again. The highway was straight, flat, unbearably hot; its heat rose through the truck's floorboards to mingle with the steam from the horses' flanks. Flies settled undisturbed on backs and rumps and in moist corners of eyes.

Occasionally the truck slowed to a stop at a sunbaked gas-station café. At these stops the horses were given hay and water, but were kept in the truck. By now they were used to the roar and smell and motion. They stood disconsolately, head to tail, swaying to keep their balance while pregnant mare jarred against pregnant mare.

As the sky began to darken the second time, the truck stopped, and after a delay of nearly an hour, the tailgate gave way to lavender sky and clean hot winds. The mares pressed back, suspicious of the offered escape, until Dragon shoved through, tested the ramp, then leaped clear of it. The stillness of the ground beneath his hooves was so welcome that at first he ignored the fact that he and the mares, who followed him from the truck, were in another high-walled corral hardly larger than the truck bed.

Hay and water appeared, and the men outside the corral disappeared. The sky went from lavender to purple to black. As the minutes passed and nothing seemed imminently threatening, some of the rigidity went out of Dragon and he allowed himself to eat and drink. The air was so filled with unfamiliar scents and small sounds that he couldn't keep his head down for more than a few seconds at a time, but he did manage to relieve the worst of the pain in his stomach.

He circled the enclosure, first at a trot, then, as the strength came back to his motion-deadened legs, at as fast a gallop as he could manage in the cramped pen. The walls were higher than his head, but he found that by rearing straight up, bracing his front hooves against the gate, and stretching his neck, he could see the distant shape of mountains.

Restless frustration kept him moving all night, from the mares who were dangerously near to foaling, to his goatlike stance at the gate. The mountains were so far and the births so near. Every instinct in his brain insisted that the mares be in the mountains, where there was cover and food, before the foaling began.

If any part of his mind acknowledged the food, water, and shelter from marauding animals that this corral afforded his mares, Dragon ignored the thought. He pawed at the gate; he turned and drove his heels into it with all the power and fury he possessed.

Early in the morning he heard voices coming from the small adobe office beyond the fence. Burr's loud tones carried clearly on the still morning air.

"Delay! How long a delay are you talking about, fellah? I got mares out there just about to foal. I got to get them up home. . . . What do you mean, can't take breeding stock out of the country? What in thunder kind of regulation is that?"

The day got hotter, and so did the voices. "Lot of hokum-pokum red tape, if you ask me. You see an American coming and right away, up goes the price. . . . Okay, how much? . . . Son of a biscuit-eater! Bunch of outlaws. Oh, all right, I guess I ain't ever going to get them home any other way. Personal check all right? Okay, now bring on your vet'nary; let's get the shots and dipping over with."

It was late afternoon when the gate opened to admit Burr and two other men, one of whom carried a large leather bag. As they made their way around the horses, Burr looked at Dragon and said, "Son, y'all are being officially exported from Mexico as a gelding and twenty-six dogs, but by thunder I got you through!"

A narrow gate on the far side of the pen was

opened, and one by one the mares were driven through it. When all the others had disappeared into the jaws of the gate, Dragon found himself the object of the chase. Shouting men and waving ropes came at him from every side. He twisted away from them, pivoted, darted, but eventually clattered through the gate.

Instantly fences crowded him on every side, inches away. A sharp jab, like the bite of a bat, stung his rump. Then a gate opened before him, and he was with his mares.

"That's all the vaccinations," someone shouted. "Ready with the dip?"

"All set."

Another gate opened, and again the mares disappeared, one at a time. When Dragon's turn came, he found himself in a long concrete alleyway. Ahead of him the floor disappeared under a pool of milky liquid that smelled somewhat like the fumes from the truck, but much stronger. It stung his eyes and burned up into the sensitive inner linings of his nostrils. He froze and tried to back away from it, but the men behind him shouted and a wire whip bit at his hindquarters.

He leaped forward. The liquid rose to his chest. A pair of arms swung a bucket toward his head, and suddenly the stinking stuff was pouring down over his face, trickling into his ears and nostrils.

Blowing furiously, Dragon plunged up and out of the pool. He stopped, shook himself off, spraying the men with a shower of milky drops, then galloped down the alley to the sanctuary of the pen beyond.

He made his way from mare to mare, assuring himself that, except for the same stench as his own coat now bore, they were unhurt. One of the mares stood apart from the group, her head low, her sides heaving. He circled her once, and knew it was too late to get to the mountains.

But before the mare's final labor began, the pen was filled with shouting, whip-wielding men, and the gate gave way to the yawning mouth of the truck bed. Dragon planted himself between the mare and the men. He squealed. He lashed at them with hooves and teeth. But in the end he was forced to follow the listless mare up into the truck where the rest of the herd waited.

The sky disappeared, the roar began again in Dragon's ears, and the floor lurched beneath him.

Several hours later, when the truck halted at an all-night truck-stop café and Burr peered through the slats at the horses, the mare was down. She lay at the rear of the truck bed, close to the tailgate, while Dragon, unable to do anything else, stood between her and the other mares and waited.

He heard a soft exclamation from the man beyond the boards; then with a clanking of chains, the

top of the tailgate fell away. Burr looked in and began to climb over.

Dragon's ears went back; his teeth gleamed in the dim light from a flashing Dr. Pepper sign. Burr paused with one leg over the tailgate. He stared into Dragon's eyes for a long moment, then said, "Okay, son. It's your show. I guess you got enough problems without me getting in there and spooking y'all."

The tailgate was closed and the truck remained still until the foal was born and the mare was on her feet again. The newborn was a black filly with snow-flake-white markings over her hindquarters.

All the next day the truck roared north, over flat land that stretched away, tan and white and dusty green, for as far as Dragon could see through his eye-level crack. It was night again when the truck made a series of turns, diminishing its speed with each turn as the road grew rougher. Finally, after humming over a brief, bumpy, metallic-sounding strip, the truck slowed to a stop, and its roar died into silence.

Chapter Nine..........

For an instant Dragon stared out at the star-frosted sky, the gently rolling plain that stretched away as far as he could see. He leaped out, his hooves scorning the ramp. Behind him the mares clattered down, tossing stiff necks and neighing with release and relief.

Dragon circled them once, then set out at a dead gallop away from the truck and the man. He breathed deeply of this strange new air. It held smells he didn't know, but they didn't bother him, not now that he was free. For the first time in days he felt a wind of his own making lift his forelock and drive it back against his ears. His hooves skimmed the grass. Over the moonlit ground he sailed as though he would never get enough of running.

Suddenly he jammed to a stop. A few yards in front of his nose was a barrier, four thin strands of black linking a line of posts. It was all but invisible in the darkness.

He trotted up to examine this thing that had stopped his flight. It looked flimsy, but when he crowded against it, it bit him. He snorted and shook his mane. He backed away and charged, intending to leap it, but as he gathered for the jump, his eyes lost the lines. Unable to gauge the height of the top wire, he wavered and turned to canter along the fence. The mares had long since tired and fallen back to graze. As he loped along, Dragon kept one eye on them, even though the man and his truck had gone.

The fence he followed was eventually crossed by another. Again Dragon turned. He found himself moving in a huge circle, with the grazing mares in its center.

At only one point was the barrier broken. There was a dirt trail here, and the strong smell of the truck. When Dragon saw the opening, he stopped, puzzled. Bridging the gap in the fence was a black hole too broad to jump. The hole was covered with iron bars placed just far enough apart that his hooves would have gone down between them if he had tried to cross. He paced back and forth, stopping several times to paw the air over the bars.

Somewhere beyond the fence and the treacherous

hole, the mountains waited—his mountains, where the mares were supposed to be.

The lesson of fence and cattle guard came easily to the mares. They had no desire to be any place but where they were. Right here they had grass, much longer and thicker than any they had ever known, and it stretched away in an inexhaustable supply all around them. Two clear streams twisted through the pasture, giving them water and shade trees. It made little difference to the mares whether or not there was a fence around this paradise.

For Dragon it was not so easy. He spent the next day galloping from fence to fence, searching the wind for the scent of the mountains. Foaling time was upon him, and he did not yet understand the dangers this new place held. Here, in this deceptively spacious, wire-bound prison, were no threats from bats, coyotes, or mountain lions, no mare-stealing, grass-coveting rival stallions, at least none so far.

The dangers Dragon tensed for as the day wore on were less tangible and far more frightening. From the south and east, far beyond the cattle guard, came the faint but constant roar and stench of the hated truck. Giant shapes thundered across the sky, blanketing the pasture with their shadows. They never actually attacked, but the strain of waiting for them to was almost harder for Dragon to bear than if they had.

But the paramount danger came from the man. Late that afternoon a pickup truck rattled over the cattle guard and crept across Dragon's pasture, creaking and rocking and spoiling the air with its smell. Burr got out and dumped a bucketful of something into a wooden box nailed to a tree. He looked at the mares and Dragon from a distance, but didn't try to come close. After he was gone, a few of the more adventurous yearlings approached the box, snuffled, and ate.

That night three mares went into labor. Two were down at the same time, and the third showed signs of following close behind. In a fever of apprehension Dragon moved from one to the other. After a wait that was nearly as exhausting for Dragon as for the mare, the first foal was born.

As the scent of blood and birth rose in the air, Dragon moved close, ready for the bats. Instead of small silent shadows, the air was suddenly filled with a ground-shaking roar, a whine that pierced Dragon's head, and huge flashing lights that bore down on him from the sky. In terror and fury he crouched near the foal. The thing thundered over his head, leaving a wake of smoke over the horses and a wake of quivering nerves beneath Dragon's skin.

The next morning when the pickup truck rattled across the cattle guard, all three new foals were nursing; but Dragon still paced from one to the other, his nerves strung to the breaking point by dangers that threatened but never quite attacked.

Burr got out of the truck and came toward the foals. Suddenly Dragon froze. Behind the man trotted a yellow creature vaguely like a coyote. At last, an enemy he could deal with. He squealed and thundered down upon the animal, who dove beneath the truck.

"Take it easy there, son. Dutchie ain't going to hurt your colts, and neither am I." But Burr was careful not to let Dragon get between him and the truck, and he contented himself with a long-distance look at the newborn foals.

Days and weeks passed, and gradually Dragon's watchfulness eased. He became as accustomed as the mares were to the planes overhead and the daily advent of the pickup truck. He didn't crowd around the wooden box to eat what the man left there, as did the mares, and it still agitated him to see the bold young fillies actually eating from the bucket while it was still in Burr's hands, but he no longer laid back his ears at the man's approach.

By midsummer Dragon's ribs, hipbones, and concave flanks had disappeared under planes of sleek muscle. Frequent splashing through sand-bottom creeks had washed away the years' collection of caked mud. The whiteness of his coat was marred by faint grass stains, and it lacked the glossy finish that oats and brushing would have given it, but even so, the little stallion was now a figure that would have caught any horseman's eye and imagination. His mane and tail held hidden stores of mats and burrs, but from a distance, which was the only way anyone ever saw him, the mane seemed to froth around a proudly arched neck, and the tail swept the grass.

Even Dragon, through tough layers of pride and belligerence, began to understand that he and his mares now had everything they needed for survival. This understanding puzzled him, angered him, left him feeling more frustrated than he had ever been in the perilous but familiar mountains. All the years of his life and all the centuries that fed his instincts had honed his senses to such a degree of sharpness that it was almost more than he could bear not to use them. From the time he was a weanling colt, he had been forced to hear better than the other horses, to sense the presence of threatening animals, to fend off the killing bats, to outrun, outfight, outsmart every threat his mountains held.

Suddenly now there were no threats. He spent his days grazing with the mares, galloping aimlessly from one fence to the other, standing at the cattle guard sifting the wind for some hint of where the mountains were.

On a beautiful green-and-gold morning Dragon stood on the crest of a low hill, looking out across the plain. Below him the mares grazed or dozed, each with her foal near by. Beyond the mares he could see the cluster of buildings from which Burr and the truck came, and far beyond that, in the blue mist of the horizon, was the faint sprawling shape of a gigantic mass of buildings.

Tiny galloping hooves brought his gaze back to the pasture. Through the long grass a jackrabbit was leaping toward him, with one of the foals close behind, her head and tail high. It was the black-and-white filly born in the back of the truck along the highway.

The rabbit shot past Dragon and under the fence, disappearing in the long grass beyond, but the filly didn't see the strands of wire in time to slow down. Her gleaming little body hit the fence. The nearest post cracked like a rifle shot, and post, filly, and wire were on the ground in a thrashing tangle.

At once Dragon was there, staring down at the filly as she bleated out her terror and struggled vainly against the wire. With each movement the barbs tore more deeply into her baby skin. The post rocked and creaked against the pull of the wire.

Dragon danced back and forth in a rage of help-lessness. When he pawed at the wire, it only wound tighter about the slim black legs, now crisscrossed with red. The mares began gathering to watch from a little distance; the filly's dam joined Dragon in his uselessness.

Suddenly the mares lifted their heads and looked over their shoulders at the pickup truck rattling toward them over the rough ground. In seconds Burr was out of the truck, wire cutters in his hand.

From force of habit Dragon planted himself between Burr and the filly. Man and horse stared hard into each other's eyes. The filly bleated again, more weakly now.

"Now you looky here, son. This ain't something you can handle by yourself, so just get out of my road." Burr's voice was granite.

Dragon hesitated, struggling to understand something that all his instincts shouted against. While he hesitated, Burr moved past him. The man was within easy striking distance of Dragon's teeth as he passed in front of the stallion, but in the confusion of dawning knowledge struggling up through old habits, Dragon stood motionless.

"Y'all got yourself in a pretty mess, young lady. Good thing for you I heard that post crack."

Dragon's ears cocked. The voice that came from the man was softer than he had known a human voice

could be. Burr wasted no motion. With half a dozen sharp snips in exactly the right places, the wire loosed its hold and was pulled gently away. Then, before the filly knew she was free, Burr scooped her up and laid her in the back of the truck.

"Don't you worry, son," he called back to Dragon. "She'll be back in a day or so." He got into the truck and slammed the door.

"And don't bother going through that hole in the fence, you hear? It's only another pasture on the other side."

Chapter Ten..............

On an afternoon a few weeks later Dragon was grazing near the cattle guard, searching out green grass among the fast-spreading burned-brown stalks. It was late July, and the sun-scorched pasture was no longer able to feed the herd. Now their food came in tight-packed bales dropped from the back of Burr's pickup truck every evening.

From the east a strong hot wind carried the smells of smoke and gasoline, smells that still brought distaste to Dragon, but no longer fear.

A movement beyond the fence caught his attention—the yellow dog. She scrambled under the fence and trotted past Dragon, her tail waving. Dragon lifted his head. The dog never came without Burr, but there was no sound of the pickup truck in the air or in the ground beneath his hooves. Then he saw

82

the riders, four of them coming across the next field from the direction of the ranch house. One of them was Burr. They came through a narrow gate near the cattle guard, a gate Dragon hadn't known was there.

At first Dragon paid little attention, but suddenly he realized the men had ropes around the necks of four of his mares and were leading them toward the gate. Trumpeting his indignation, he galloped toward Burr. He tried to crowd in between Burr's horse and the mare the man led, but a quirt smacked him sharply across the nose. Startled, he fell back.

They were at the gate. By practiced maneuvering, Burr held Dragon off while the others got through. As Dragon made a final lunge at the mare, and caught another stinging swat, the gate clanked shut. One mare, an old one who had been in the herd since before Dragon was born, turned to look back at him. Perplexed and angry, he churned back and forth along the fence, his eyes fastened on the disappearing mares.

The men came back and chose four more. These, like the first four, were either pintos or duns. Most had foals at their sides, and the foals were allowed to follow as the mares were led away. Again Dragon tried to crowd in, tried to drive the mares back. Again he was left to stare after them as they disappeared toward the house.

For the next several days Dragon was filled with

a restless, frustrated energy. He cantered the length and width of his eighty acres, testing the breeze and searching the low hills for his missing mares. The humiliation of having nearly half of his herd taken from him, after all of the years and all of the battles he had fought to retain them, burned inside him. When Burr came each day to bring hay or salt blocks, Dragon galloped away from the truck. With smoldering eyes he watched his remaining mares cluster around the man, taking the food he brought and allowing him to touch them, to buckle tiny halters around the foals' heads.

Then one day it was the large stock truck that came over the cattle guard instead of the pickup. Dragon watched from a safe distance as Burr pulled the tailgate bolts, extended the ramp, and walked inside the truck. Suddenly Dragon's ears stiffened; his head lifted. A gleaming blood-bay mare came down the ramp, and behind her another and another. Blacks, bright bays, chestnuts, and sorrels, the mares poured from the truck and fanned out across his pasture.

Dragon thundered over to them. He circled the new mares; he danced, snorted, shook his mane, nipped at their necks. There were more than twenty of them, all purebred Hackneys, Welsh, Arabian, or quarter horses, all carefully chosen for the qualities which, in combination with Dragon's spirit and toughness and appaloosa background, would produce what Burr wanted.

Dragon understood nothing of selective breeding; he knew only that in some way the man had made up for taking Dragon's own mares. Anger still lingered inside him at being forced to let the man decide what mares he would and would not have, but now he didn't mind quite so much.

He circled the new mares and, with a few well-placed nips, drove them toward the others. He stopped once and sent a ringing neigh down to the man who stood watching beside the truck.

Burr laughed and waved him away.

Days and weeks and months passed with treadmill monotony for Dragon. He watched over his increased herd, but there was nothing to guard them from. The fences that kept the horses in also kept out all other animals except for jackrabbits and the yellow dog.

Imperceptibly Dragon's senses began to lose their edge. The keenness of his ears and nostrils, which had saved his life and his herd time and again in the mountains, was gradually becoming dulled by the roar of jets, the gasoline smells, the lack of necessity for their keenness. Although he spent endless hours galloping across the pasture, uselessness dulled his days.

As the months of winter came and went, Dragon began to feel a renewed urge toward the south, toward mountains. The mares grew heavy with foal, and Dragon became increasingly restless. He spent more and more of his time at the narrow gate beside the cattle guard.

With the coming of spring the pasture turned from tan to green. The horses no longer needed Burr's hay, but the man came each afternoon anyway. He and the yellow dog moved among the mares while Dragon watched with decreasing suspicion. He seldom bothered to move away from the mares now when the man came, but he still avoided the touch of Burr's hand. Several times Burr tried in a casual way to slip a soft white rope halter over Dragon's face, but when the horse shied away, Burr didn't press the matter.

On a night in late spring Dragon stood at the gate beside the cattle guard, watching the line of flashing lights far to the south. From his left came sounds of music, many voices laughing, occasionally the booming voice Dragon recognized as Burr's. The noises had been going on for some time now, accenting the stillness of the night-blackened pasture. Dragon pawed at the gate post, and his hoof made a soft chunking sound against the wood.

He turned to look at the mares. Even in the moonlight they showed the bulk of their annual payment of dues to the man who fed them, the foals soon to be born.

The old restlessness was in Dragon tonight, stronger than it had been for many weeks. The instincts that told him to take the mares up into the mountains could not be stilled by the months of security here. Not tonight. Something was wrong, and it wouldn't be right until the mares were in the Den of the Dragons Canyon for the foaling season.

As the uneasiness and frustration built higher and higher in him, Dragon pawed harder at the gate. It was made of barbed wire like the rest of the fence, four strands that ended at a pole fastened to the gatepost by a rusted chain.

Again and again his hoof struck out at the posts, and as he pawed, he gathered excitement from the rhythm of the movement. When the narrower post finally cracked away, its two halves falling from the loops of chain, he was startled.

He stared at the opening. He raised his head and searched the wind for traces of his mountains. He looked back at the mares.

Chapter Eleven.........

The new mares, unaccustomed to being herded, were harder to drive than his old ones had been. They wandered away from him, meandered back toward where they had been grazing, ignored the opening in the fence. Dragon worked patiently, then impatiently, until they were finally through the gate and moving south.

He kept them on the narrow dirt road that led away from the cattle guard, but even on this trail, where the going was smooth, it took all his energy to keep the foolish mares bunched together and traveling in the right direction. They were just settling down and beginning to move well when the dirt track became concrete that jarred Dragon's leg bones and offended his nostrils. The mares didn't like it either, but with constant heading off and nipping, Dragon managed to keep them moving.

Suddenly two bright lights were bearing down on Dragon from in front of the mares. They had appeared so abruptly that for an instant Dragon almost wheeled and bolted away. But the lights stopped moving toward them. Something blared loudly, and voices shouted, but the shadowy truck-like thing behind the lights stood still. Dragon headed the lead mare off to the edge of the road and around the noisy object.

Before the mares had quieted, before the terror in Dragon could melt, the concrete road was cut off in front of him by a high striped barricade. Dragon stopped. He looked from side to side, and as he looked, he was filled with a greater fear than he had ever known. On either side of him the concrete stretched away, broad and blue-white with an unearthly brilliance.

Suddenly new lights blazed. The air was torn with screeching, roaring, thudding. A mare screamed. A giant sun loomed before Dragon's eyes, exploded in his head.

A tide of blackness swept him up and carried him gently down through endless canyons. Mountain passes, suns, vague shapes, revolved before his eyes. He sank without a struggle beneath the water of the

mud lake in the foothills of his mountains, and when he washed up on the shore, he heard Burr's voice.

"Wait, officer. I think he's just stunned. Hold off a minute."

Before the earth had ceased its turning, Dragon was struggling to his feet. He stood, head down, legs braced wide against the rocking of the ground.

Close to his head stood Burr and a man with a gun. Burr's voice was weary as he said, "This one's okay, officer. Take care of them two mares."

As his vision cleared, Dragon saw a wall of lights on either side, steady white ones and flashing red ones. Burr's stock truck was near by, and Dragon could hear the rustling of his mares' hooves from within its black box. In the eerie blue light on the broad expanse of concrete in front of him were the still forms of two mares and, on the grassy shoulder beyond, the smaller shape of a black-and-white filly. The barbed-wire scars on her slender legs were hidden now by fresh blood. Two cars and a large truck stood in the lighted arena too, canted in unnatural angles and surrounded by blood and glass.

Dragon was only dimly aware of the rope around his neck, of Burr's hands touching his head and legs.

"Don't look like anything's broke. Can you move, son? How you can get yourself hit by a double-bottom semi and come through it in one piece is beyond me, I swear."

A shot split the air, and after a long pause another and another. The man with the gun came to stand beside Burr and Dragon.

"Can you manage this one, Mr. Burr?"

"Yes, thanks, officer. I'm sure sorry about all this. Just a blessing no one in any of them cars got hurt! Now, if you got all the information you need, I'd like to get this guy back home and make sure he's okay. Thanks for calling me."

"You bet. One of our men will be around in a day or so, with the accident reports and all that red tape, but for now we've done all we can. You go ahead home and see to your horse."

The rope tightened around his neck, but there was nothing left in Dragon that wanted to fight it. He took a step forward, then another. Slowly, as numbness gave way to pain, he made his way beside the man, up the ramp and into the truck where his mares stood, pressed together in the blackness.

At the top of the ramp they stood, Burr and Dragon, looking back at the men who struggled to drag the mares' bodies out of the way of traffic. When Burr spoke, there was anger in his voice, but it was overlaid with sorrow, even compassion.

"Son, that was an expensive lesson you just learned. I hope you don't forget it."

His hand rested on Dragon's withers for a moment before Dragon shivered his skin and moved away from the touch.

Through the growing awareness of pain in Dragon's mind, another awareness was rising. It had begun to germinate in the Montenegro corral and had stirred again, more strongly, the day he watched Burr free the black-and-white filly from the barbed wire.

For months his mind had understood that, in this world of baled hay and barbed wire, it was the man who must provide for him and for the mares the food and protection that had always been his job. Now, finally, his heart was able to accept this understanding.

He let his head rest against the top board of the tailgate, and when Burr's hand again touched his neck, he didn't move away.

The Legacy ....

For three years after his capture Dragon lived on a ranch near Dallas and sired the scores of outstanding POA ponies who were to bring him fame. These sons and daughters of Dragon bore not only his appaloosa markings but also the inner stamp of the Dragon bloodline, a courage and stamina and intelligence that made them unexcelled in the show-ring and in the hearts of their young owners.

As for Dragon himself, at an age when most horses would be considered old, the little white stallion began a new career, a career that called for all the swiftness and sharpness of instinct that kept him alive through his years in the mountains. Under the loving hand of a fifteen-year-old Iowa boy, Dragon was broken to ride and learned the demanding art of Western performance competition. Racing against the country's finest young POAs, at the age of fifteen he won an International Performance Championship.

Civilization will someday put an end to the wild horses of Michoacán, but they will not disappear completely. In stables and corrals and backyard pony pens across the continent, the spirit of the Barbs shines in the eyes of small freckled horses whose pedigrees bear the name *Dragon*.

F
HAL

Hall, Lynn

13,220

A horse called
Dragon

DATE			

13,220
265787

© THE BAKER & TAYLOR CO.